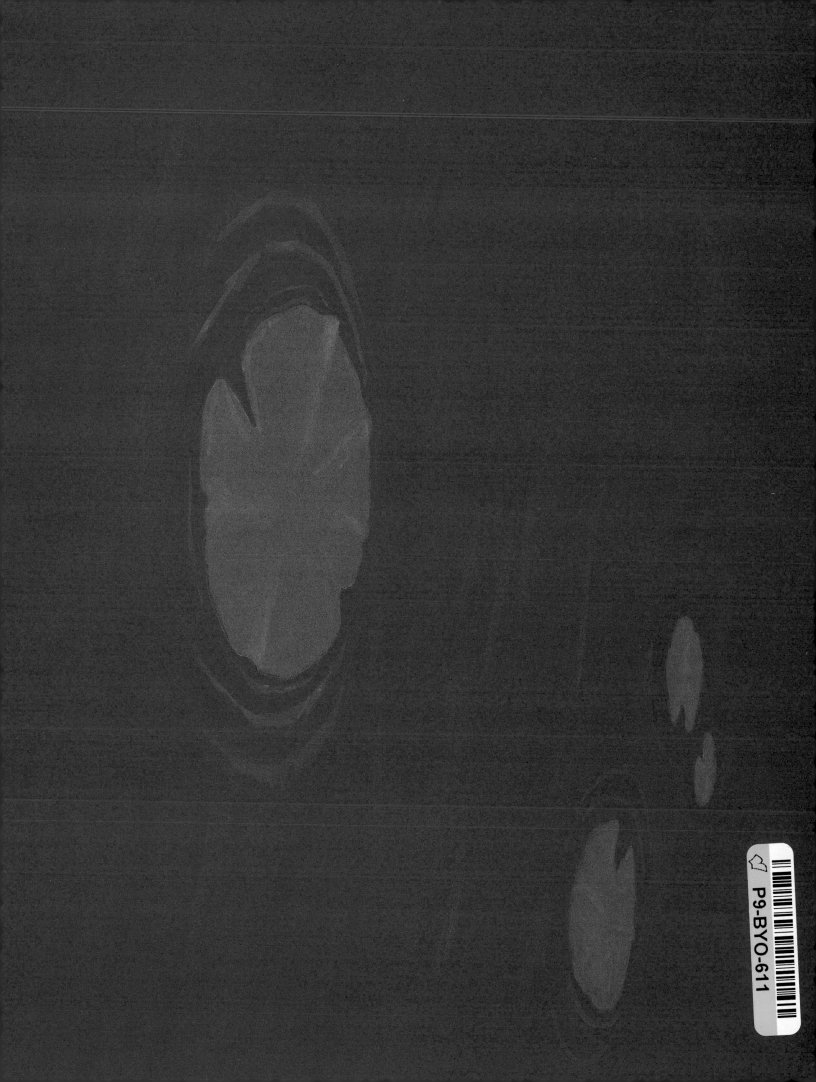

A Frog Thing

by Eric Drachman

illustrated by James Muscarello

Kidwick books

Kidwick
books

www.kidwick.com

Copyright 2005 Kidwick Books LLC

Publisher's Cataloging-In-Publication Data
(Prepared by The Donohue Group, Inc.)

Drachman, Eric.

A frog thing / by Eric Drachman ; illustrated by James Muscarello.

p. : ill. ; cm. + 1 sound disc.

Frank wasn't satisfied with doing ordinary frog things. He wanted to
fly. But he was a frog, and frogs can't fly. Frank flaps, jumps, runs,
leaps, and dives until he finally finds his place in the pond.

ISBN-13: 978-0-9703809-3-7

ISBN-10: 0-9703809-3-3

1. Frogs—Juvenile fiction. 2. Self-acceptance—Juvenile fiction.
3. Children's audiobooks. 4. Frogs—Fiction. 5. Self-acceptance—
Fiction. 6. Audiobooks. I. Muscarello, James. II. Title.

PS3554.R14 F73 2005
813.6/083

2005901999

Voices on CD (alphabetically):

Benjamin Drachman (Frank), Eric Drachman (Narrator, Dad, Various Frogs),
Katharine Gibson Dayan (Mom), Pamela Vanderway (Mother Bird)

Various frogs by: Carlos Calleja, Julia Drachman, Rebecca Drachman, and Chloe Sachs

Excerpted recordings from Scherzo by Gregor Piatigorsky,
The Swan by Camille Saint-Saëns,
and Cello Concerto in E Minor, Op.85 by Edward Elgar
from CDs entitled A frog he went a-Courting and Infinity
courtesy of The Piatigorsky Foundation and Evan Drachman
Evan Drachman, cello; Richard Dowling, piano.

Text design and layout by Andrew Leman and Kate Cardoza. Set in Kidegorey.
Color management & production by Andrew Behla.
Illustrations rendered with gouache paint, colored pencil, and pastel
on illustration and colored matte board.

Printed in Korea

Distributed by National Book Network

Published in Los Angeles, CA U.S.A. by Kidwick Books LLC

Frank wanted to fly.

But he was a frog.

And frogs can't fly.

Frank was different, though.

Special.

Aerodynamic.

"You can do whatever you set your mind to, Frankie," his parents had promised.

So Frank set his mind to flying...

...but it was more like falling than flying.

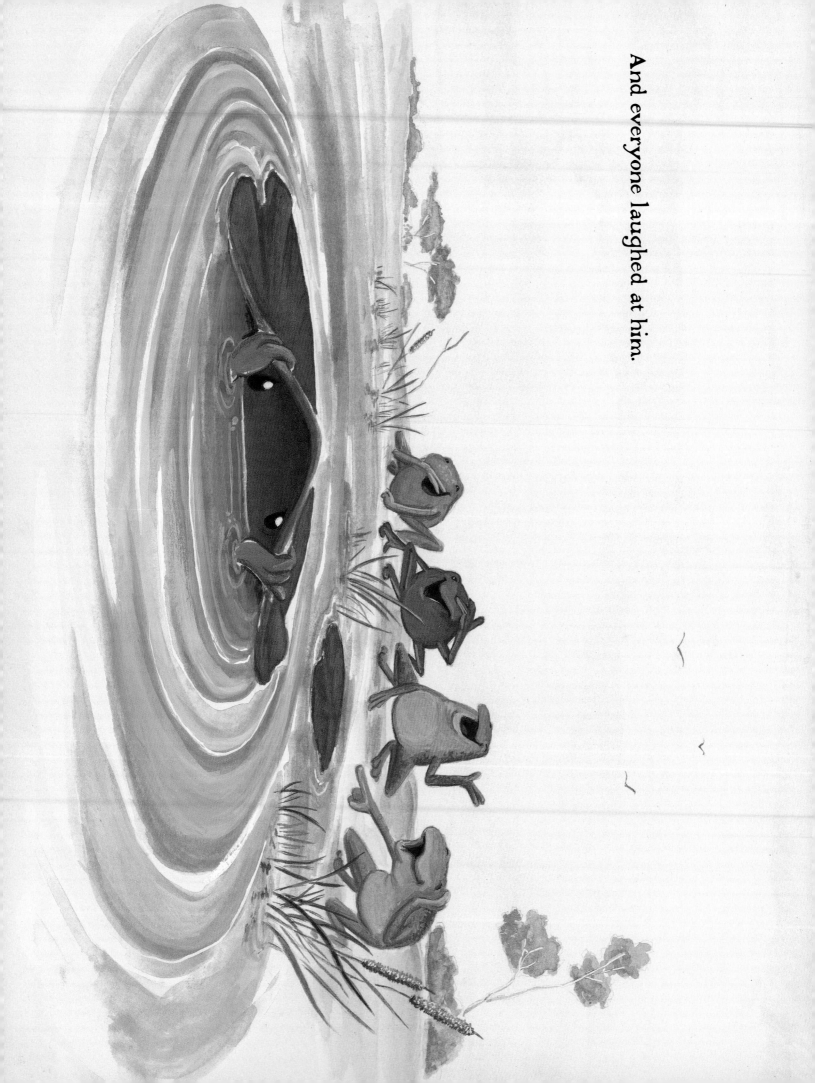

And everyone laughed at him.

Tired and discouraged, Frank buried his head in his big webbed feet.

And that's how Frank's parents found him.

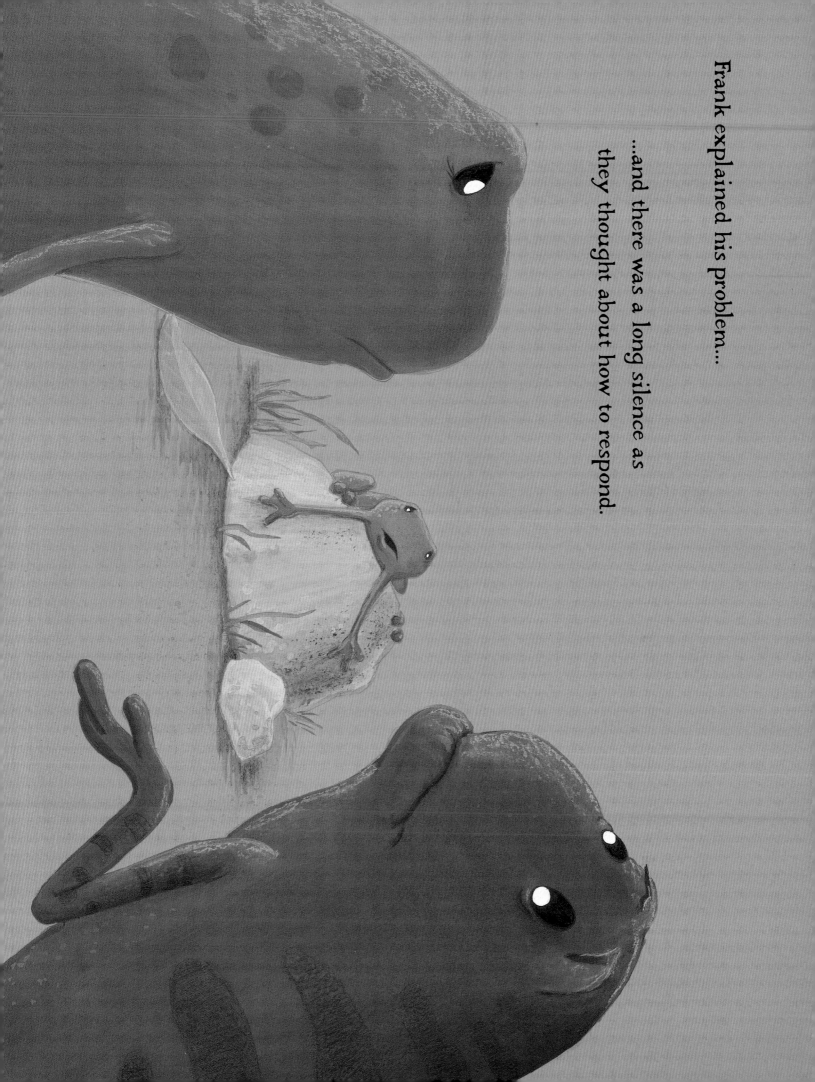

Frank explained his problem...

...and there was a long silence as they thought about how to respond.

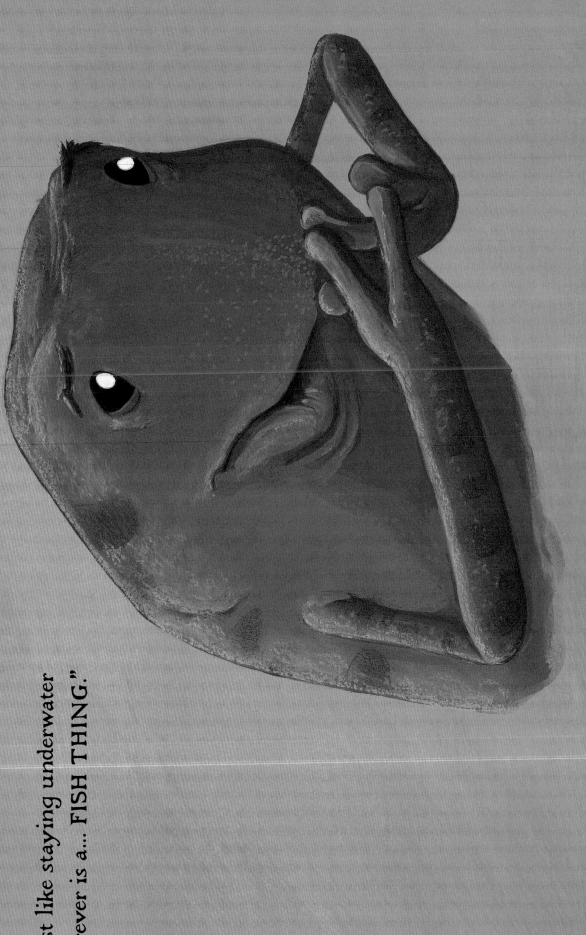

"Frankie..." started Frank's dad, finally, "when we said you could do anything you set your mind to, we meant any... FROG THING.

See, flying is a... BIRD THING...

just like staying underwater forever is a... FISH THING."

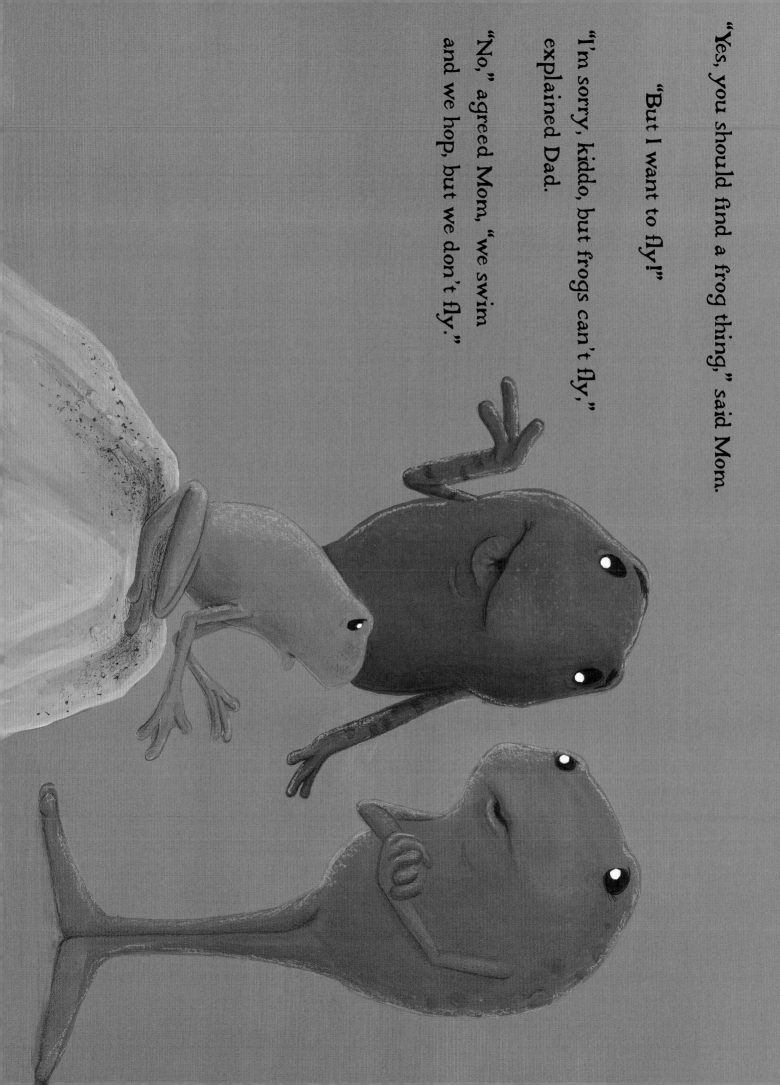

"Yes, you should find a frog thing," said Mom.

"But I want to fly!"

"I'm sorry, kiddo, but frogs can't fly," explained Dad.

"No," agreed Mom, "we swim and we hop, but we don't fly."

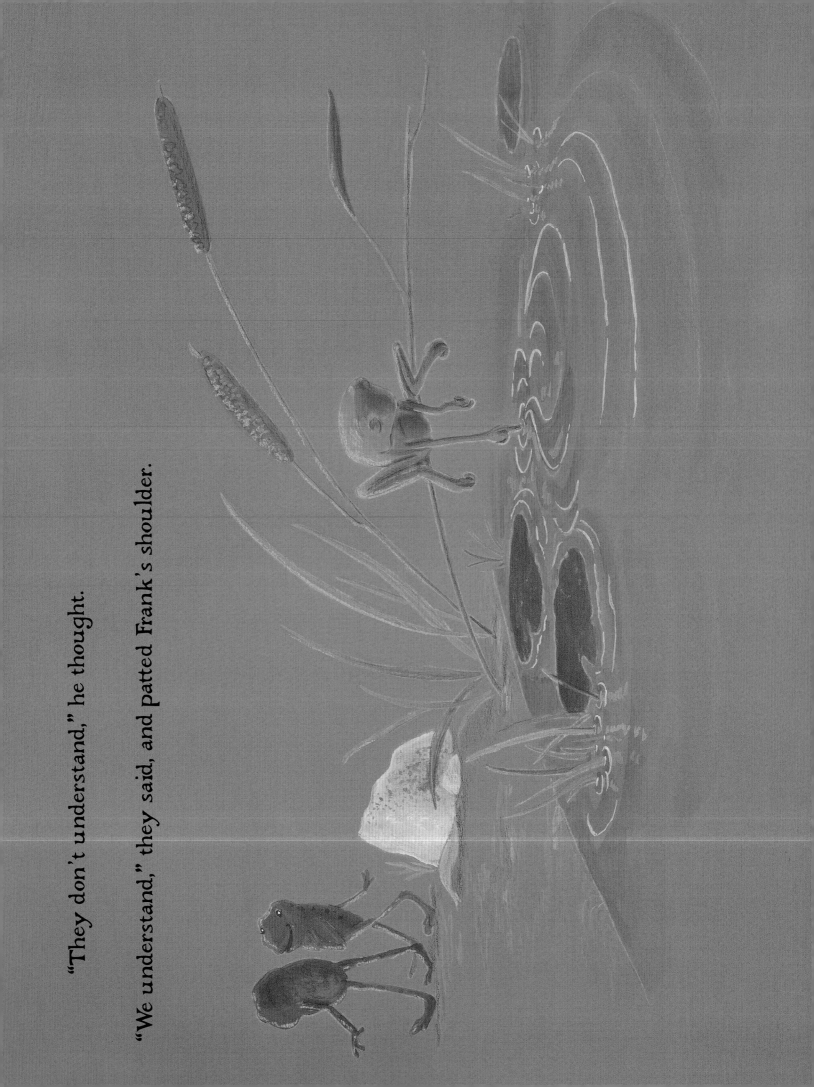

"They don't understand," he thought.

"We understand," they said, and patted Frank's shoulder.

Frank sat in the dark, still sad, but growing more determined.

"I'll show them," he thought.
"I'll learn to fly, and I'll fly right over the pond!"

He jumped and ran

and leapt and dove.

He flapped

and flapped

and flapped...

...and finally just *flopped* on top of a leaf to rest. He soaked his sore feet and hung his heavy head until...

...*SPLASH!*

Something crashed into the water and started to sink.

Frank leapt into action.

"It's a little baby bird!" he thought.

He swooped down...

swept her up...

and swam her back to shore.

The nervous mother bird hugged her baby tight.

Her baby coughed, then wheezed, then opened her eyes... safe and warm in her mother's wings.

The mother bird turned and kissed Frank
right on the cheek. He was very surprised
and a little embarrassed.

"Thank you, *thank you!*" she chirped.

"What a great swimmer you are!
How can I ever repay you?"

"Oh, it was nothing, Ma'am," said Frank,
for he was a very polite and modest frog.

"Please. I want to do something for you. Anything."

"Well…" suggested Frank,
"I really really want to fly."

"But, frogs don't fly," said the mother bird.

"I know," admitted Frank.

"And you still want to fly?"

Frank shrugged. "I've set my mind to it."

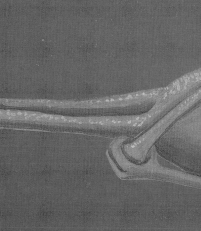

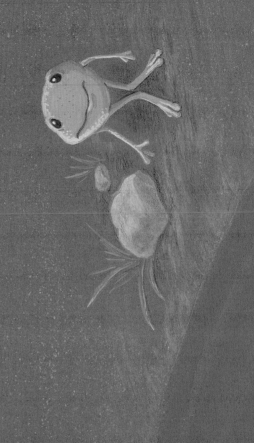

She looked in his eyes... then flew off in a flutter.

"Wait here," she cried. "I'll be right back!"

And she did come back ~ with another bird,
and a twig between them.

"Grab on!" she called.

Before he knew it, they were high above the trees. The morning sun streamed through the sky, and the wind whistled over Frank's slick green skin.

It was a little scary at first, but soon he relaxed, as they glided and rose and swooped and dove.

Everyone hurried to see Frank fly.

They watched from the bank as he
and the birds passed high overhead.

"This is no ordinary frog thing!"
observed Frank's mom.

When their flight was finished, the mother bird pulled Frank close.

"You are a very special frog," she said, and with a whoosh of her wings, flew back to her nest.

Breathless, Frank waved, "Thank you!"

"*Thank you so much.*"

Frank hopped home, somehow lighter than before.

On his way, he met his folks.

"Frankie, we saw you up there!" Mom beamed.

"Fantastic!" croaked Dad. "You *can* do anything you set your mind to!"

"Anything," agreed Mom.

"Well... any *frog* thing, maybe," Frank explained. "The birds were the ones flying. I was just holding on.

But I *do* think I could be one of the great swimmers!"

His parents smiled proudly as Frank joined his friends in the pond.

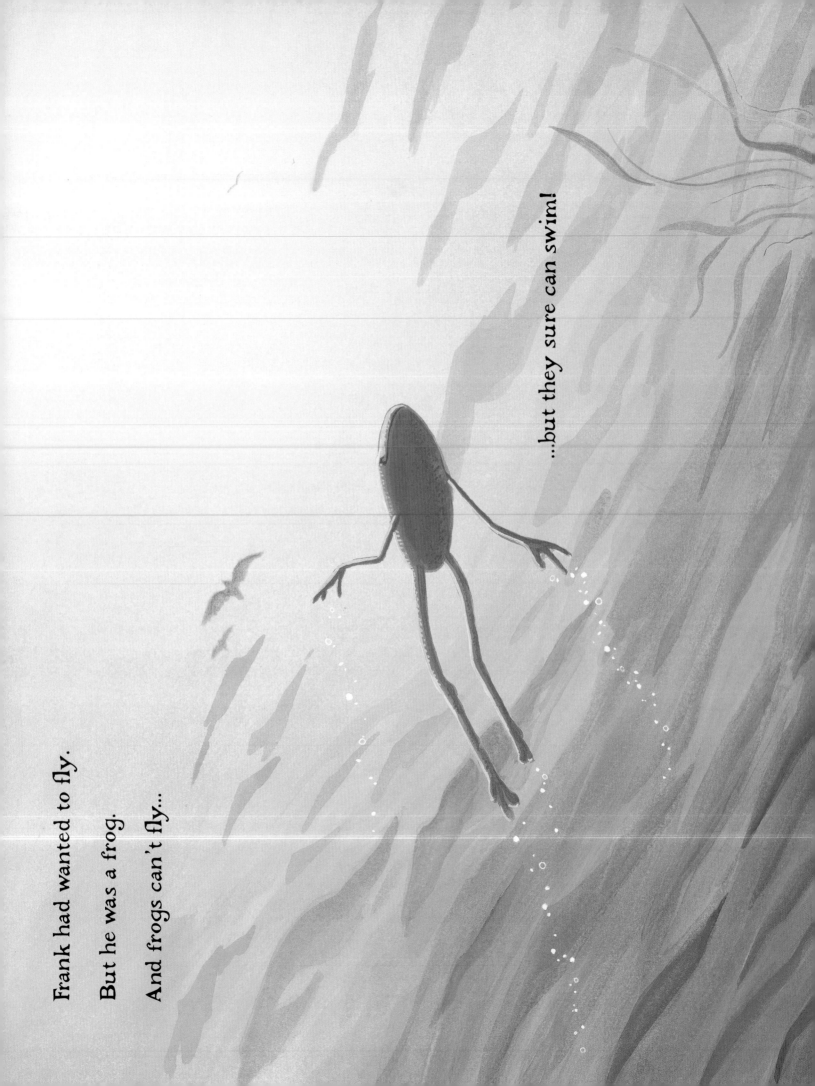

Frank had wanted to fly.

But he was a frog.

And frogs can't fly...

...but they sure can swim!

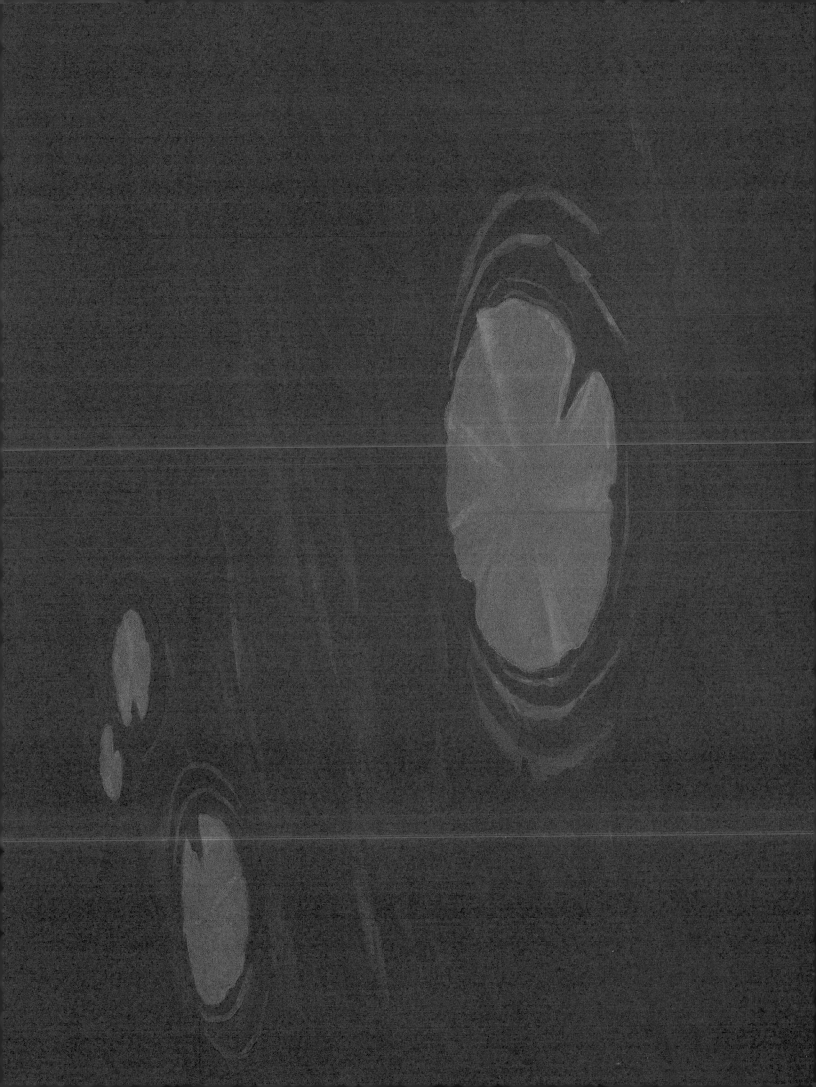